FAERIEGROUND

Promise

Book Twelve

BY BETH BRACKEN AND KAY FRASER
ILLUSTRATED BY ODESSA SAWYER

STONE ARCH BOOKS
a capstone imprint

FAERIEGROUND IS PUBLISHED BY
STONE ARCH BOOKS
A CAPSTONE IMPRINT
1710 ROE CREST DRIVE
NORTH MANKATO, MINNESOTA 56003
WWW.CAPSTONEPUB.COM

LIBRARY OF CONGRESS CATALOGING-IN-PUBLICATION DATA

BRACKEN, BETH, AUTHOR.

  PROMISE / BY BETH BRACKEN AND KAY FRASER ; ILLUSTRATED BY
ODESSA SAWYER.

     PAGES CM. -- (FAERIEGROUND ; 12)

  SUMMARY: THE FATE OF FAERIEGROUND HANGS IN THE BALANCE--
AND ANDRIA, MOTHER OF LUCY AND CARO, IS THE KEY TO WHETHER
THE KINGDOMS WILL FALL TO THE CROWS, OR BE UNITED IN PEACE.

  ISBN 978-1-4342-9188-2 (LIBRARY BINDING) -- ISBN 978-1-4342-9192-9
(PBK.)

1. FAIRIES--JUVENILE FICTION. 2. BEST FRIENDS--JUVENILE FICTION.
3. MAGIC--JUVENILE FICTION. 4. MOTHERS AND DAUGHTERS--
JUVENILE FICTION. [1. FAIRIES--FICTION. 2. BEST FRIENDS--FICTION.
3. FRIENDSHIP--FICTION. 4. MAGIC--FICTION. 5. SECRETS--FICTION. 6.
MOTHERS AND DAUGHTERS--FICTION.]

I. FRASER, KAY, AUTHOR. II. SAWYER, ODESSA, ILLUSTRATOR. III.
TITLE. IV.

SERIES: BRACKEN, BETH. FAERIEGROUND ; [BK. 12]

  PZ7.B6989PR 2014

  813.6--DC23

                         2014002993

BOOK DESIGN BY K. FRASER

ALL PHOTOS © SHUTTERSTOCK WITH THESE EXCEPTIONS:
AUTHOR PORTRAIT © K FRASER AND ILLUSTRATOR PORTRAIT
© ODESSA SAWYER

PRINTED IN THE UNITED STATES OF AMERICA.
009846R

"Those who don't believe in magic
will never find it."

– Roald Dahl

For Etta, my daughter. —— BB
To the love of my life and best friend, JB —— KF

The baby grew into a young woman,
and she hated her mother.

She felt left behind and abandoned. She felt betrayed. She felt alone in the faerieground. She didn't have a friend in the world.

Chapter 1

Lucy

I follow Caro and Soli up a long staircase.

Kheelan is behind us, making sure no one else knows where we're going.

At the top of the stairs is a room full of flowers. Up here, it's hard to believe a battle still rages down below.

Outside the window, the sky keeps getting darker.

We just stand there, watching.

"This is so scary," I say, finally, breaking the silence.

Caro nods.

"I'm not afraid," Kheelan says. "How much damage can one human woman do? Andria won't defeat all of these warriors."

Soli frowns. "I'm afraid too," she says. "I've been reading Andria's journal, from when she was here. And—"

She looks at me and bites her lip. Then she says, "I'm sorry, Lucy, for what I'm going to say."

"It's okay," I say. "I think I already know. You're going to say that she was crazy. Is crazy."

Soli nods slowly. "It's like she lost her mind," she says. "She was so obsessed with the faerieground. And when she got here and Georg fell in love with her—"

"She got even crazier," I finish. Soli and I stare at each other.

"But what I don't understand is why it's so dangerous for her to be here," Caro says. "What's the big deal?"

I lean on the windowsill. "I don't get that part either," I admit. "But Motherbird—"

Just then, there's a gentle knock on the door. Caro opens it, and Motherbird herself walks in.

"We were just talking about you," Soli says, smiling.

"I know," Motherbird says. She settles herself onto a bench. "I came to answer the questions that I know the four of you have."

"Tell us why my mother is so dangerous," I say, sitting down next to Motherbird.

She sighs. "She herself isn't dangerous," she says slowly. "Georg is dangerous."

"So why does it matter if Andria is here?" Kheelan asks.

"She was beloved in the kingdom," Motherbird says. "She wanted to be faerie more than anything else in the world, and she would— and will—stop at nothing to become the faerie queen of the Crows."

"Is there a way for her to become a faerie?"
Soli asks quietly.

Motherbird nods.

"What is it?" Caro asks. "I thought that was
impossible. Everyone has always said it was
impossible."

"I know you asked to become full faerie,"
Motherbird tells her, and Kheelan and Soli and
I stare at Caro.

"You did?" Kheelan asks. "Why?"

Caro snorts. "Well, wouldn't you try everything?" she asks. "If you were half-human, I mean? And everyone knew it?"

"No," Soli says. She reaches over and pats Caro's hand. "But I understand. Not quite fitting into either world."

"Is that why you're the Betrayer?" Kheelan asks. "Because you would try anything, betray anyone, say anything, to find out how to become full faerie?"

Caro snorts. "This isn't about me," she says.

"What it takes to become full faerie is known," Motherbird says.

Caro stares at her. "No it isn't," she says.

"Yes, it is," Motherbird says gently.

"Everyone has always told me it was impossible," Caro says. "Impossible. Completely impossible. Out of the question."

"I know," Motherbird says. "And the fact remains, everyone has lied to you."

She gestures out the window.

"She's here," she says calmly.

The five of us stare down at the battleground.

The crowd of faeries slowly parts, and a figure in blue makes her way through them.

"My mother," Caro whispers.

My mother.

"She's so small," I say. "She doesn't look like she could hurt anyone."

"I don't think she wants to hurt anyone," Motherbird says carefully. "But she will not let not wanting to be evil stop her, when it comes down to it. She wants to be faerie—to be the faerie queen of the Equinox kingdom—more than she wants to be good."

"So what is the secret?" I ask. "What makes a human become faerie?"

Motherbird sighs. "The reason we keep this a secret," she says, "is because of what it takes— what the magic requires."

"Are you going to tell us, or not?" Kheelan

asks. "I can tell it's important for us to know

what it takes."

She nods. "You're right," Motherbird says.

"What it takes—what the magic demands—is

the kingdom's necklace—the source of its

power—and the blood of a halfling."

Chapter 2

Soli

The blood of a halfling.

"That means me," I say.

"Or me," Caro says.

We stare at each other. Motherbird stares out the window.

"Andria is in the palace now," Kheelan says, gazing down into the courtyard, still full of faeries. "We need to protect you both."

"We need to protect all of you," Motherbird says. She stands up. "Stay here." Then she leaves, her red coat trailing behind her.

"Should I go talk to her?" Lucy asks. "To my mother?"

Kheelan shakes his head. "Wearing the Equinox pendant? No," he says.

"I don't understand something," Caro admits. "Why would it matter if a necklace were part of the spell? A necklace is just a necklace. I don't even know what they're talking about."

"That's not true," Lucy says. "First of all, there are seven necklaces."

I nod. "Roseland's is part of my crown," I explain. "But Andria had it before that."

Lucy pulls a blue pendant out of her shirt. "And this one belongs to the Crows."

Caro narrows her eyes. "I've never seen that before," she says.

"It was lost," Kheelan says. "So the story goes."

"I found it in a closet, the day Soli sent us home," Lucy says. "So I guess it was lost. But not lost that well."

Then I understand. The Crows thought their own pendant was lost, so they sent Andria home with Roseland's.

"They knew she needed one of the necklaces for part of the spell," I say slowly. "That's why Andria had mine."

"That gives me the creeps," Lucy says.

"But they know I have it now," I say.

"Yes," Caro says. "You even convinced my father to give it back to you."

"Your people," Kheelan seethes.

"Stop it," I say. Kheelan's eyes open wide.

"She's on our side," I say. "She can't betray us. She's a halfling too."

Caro and I stare at each other. We are both not quite human, not quite faerie. At least someone understands.

"You're the only halfling at risk, Soli," Kheelan says. "If they just needed any halfling, they would've killed Caro when she was a baby."

And I know he is right.

"She couldn't have," Lucy says quietly, looking at her half-sister. "She loved you too much." Then she looks at me. "But she loves you, too, Soli."

I laugh. "Loves me enough to raise me up until she could send me back to the faerieground," I mutter. "Loves me enough to kill me."

"I won't betray you," Caro whispers. She reaches over and squeezes my hand.

Beneath the window, the faerie army retreats. The sky is a deep, dark shade of blue.

We hear shouting from downstairs, but we can't understand the words. I hear Andria's voice, and Georg's. And Motherbird's.

And then it is silent.

"Motherbird is gone," Kheelan whispers. He points to the window.

Outside, a red bird soars past the castle and into the sky.

Chapter 3

Lucy

The four of us head back to
Roseland as soon as night falls.

Caro doesn't stop to pack anything in her room. She just leaves, carrying only her bow and quiver. She doesn't turn her head in the direction of our mother's voice in the throne room, the sound of her father laughing with our mother. She doesn't even turn around when we reach the gardens at the edge of the castle grounds. She just keeps moving forward.

We have to walk for two days. Jonn meets us in the woods. Finally, we make it back. At the palace, Soli, Caro, and I walk up the stairs to the rooms where Queen Calandra lived. We fall onto the soft couches and sleep.

When I wake up, a whole day has passed. Caro and Soli are gone.

They've left a note: *Come to the throne room when you can.* I splash water on my face and head downstairs.

When I open the heavy doors, I see Kheelan, Soli, and Caro gathered at the table where I met the other faerie leaders before the war began. It looks like a study table in the library at school, the way they're hunched together over books and papers, but I know they're not cramming for a quiz or researching an essay.

Not for the first time, I think this adventure is too much for me. I used to be a normal girl, and here I am, the daughter of a woman who wants to murder my best friend as part of a spell to become a faerie queen.

Not for the first time, I wish I'd never come to this place.

Chapter 4

Soli

We've only been back at the palace in Roseland for a day, but already I feel overwhelmed.

I'm no queen. But I know I have to act like one. So as soon as I wake up, after napping for a few hours, I go to Jonn and Kheelan's rooms. Caro and Lucy are still asleep. Kheelan answers the door, and his eyes soften when he sees me. "Hello," he says, pulling me by the hand into their main room.

But I pull my hand back. When his face looks hurt, I try to look reassuring. "I'm here on business," I say.

He knows that his father is the Queen's main advisor. "I'll get my father," he says.

Jonn comes out of his room, looking tired. He must have been waiting in the woods for us after the battle. Who knows if he even slept.

"Hello, Queen Soledad," he says, bowing lightly. "I hope you were able to rest."

"Hi, Jonn," I say. "I need your help. I need to figure out what to do next."

We sit down at their modest dining table. Kheelan serves me a cup of tea. It tastes like rose petals and grass.

"Have you heard about Motherbird?" Jonn asks.
I shake my head. "She is gone," he says. "Another
Ladybird, Elsain, has taken her place."

"Was it Andria?" I whisper.

"No," Jonn says. "Georg. But I'm sure Andria
had something to do with it."

"Is Elsain on our side?" I ask.

He nods. "Motherbird knew this was coming,
of course," he says. "She was prepared, and she
chose her successor carefully."

"Motherbird was amazing," I say quietly.

Jonn smiles. "She was," he says. "But I'll never understand why she brought you to Andria, knowing what we know now."

"It was a spell," I tell him. "I read about it in a book I found in the Crow palace." Then I tell him about the secret room and the book where the Crows wrote their plan.

Jonn shakes his head when I'm done. "They're worse than we thought," he says.

"They're evil," Kheelan adds.

"They just want power," I say. "And they have a terrible king."

"Was he awful to you?" Kheelan asks, reaching across the table to take my hand.

I think. Was he awful? He fed me, clothed me, trained me. He praised me. He trusted me. He was cruel to his daughter. He would have gladly killed me.

"I don't trust him," I say finally. "At all."

"And with Andria back, there's not a Crow in the world we can trust," Jonn says.

Kheelan shakes his head. "We can trust Caro," he says. "She's a betrayer, but—"

"But she's been waiting to find the right side to be on," I finish for him. We smile at each other across the table.

"So what is your plan?" Jonn asks me. "What do we do?"

"I came here to ask you that," I admit.

"What does your blood tell you?" he asks.

"What do you hear when you listen?"

And while it's a strange question, I know what he means. I close my eyes and listen.

I listen to my heart. I hear my heartbeat, pulsing my blood through my body. I feel my veins thriving. The faerie blood mixed with the human blood.

And then I know what we have to do.

What I have to do.

Chapter 5

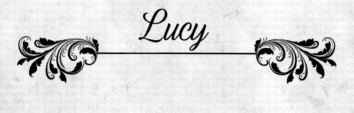

Lucy

In the throne room, Soli turns around and sees me.

"You're awake!" she says. "Come sit down.
We'll fill you in."

I join them at the table, and Caro passes
me a cup of hot tea and a plate of cookies.
I suddenly realize that I'm starving. "Thank
you," I say, before cramming a cookie into my
mouth.

"We have a plan," Soli tells me.

"But you're not going to like it," Caro adds.
When Kheelan and Soli glare at her, she says,
"What? She's not going to."

"You have to go back to the Crows," Soli

explains.

I stop chewing and stare at them. "What?

Why?" I ask.

"Because you're the only one who's safe to go,"

Kheelan says. "I'll bring you there tomorrow."

"What am I doing there?" I ask.

"You are convincing them to rejoin our

kingdoms," Soli says.

"There's no way they'll agree to that," I say. "It was hard enough for Jonn to convince the peaceful leaders to fight the Crows."

"And Motherbird is gone now," Soli says. "It will be hard to convince any of them to join."

"Why would my mother agree to that?" I ask. "She wants to be queen of the Crows, remember? She doesn't care if the kingdoms are reunited."

Soli and Kheelan look at each other. "We will make a deal with her," Soli says.

"What kind of deal?" I ask.

"It's a sort of trade," Soli says. "If they join with us, we'll give them what they want."

"What do you mean?" I ask, but I already know.

"The blood of a halfling," Soli says. She holds out her wrist.

I want to cry, but I don't. Then I remember something. "What about the necklace?" I say. "She needs a necklace too. You can't reunite the kingdoms without a necklace."

Soli smiles. "It turns out that once the kingdoms reunite, the necklaces still exist. Or they turn into one necklace, or something. But there's always a necklace. So we'll give her that."

"No, you won't," comes another voice.

We all turn. A woman dressed in red stands in the entrance to the throne room.

Soli stands. "You must be Elsain," she says. "Welcome to Roseland."

"What do you mean about the necklace?" Caro asks. "Why won't it work? They agree to unite the kingdoms, and we give them the necklace once that's done."

"Because the necklace is the heartsource of the faerieground," Elsain explains calmly. "If it is destroyed, we are all destroyed. That's part of why we were split to begin with, millennia ago. Because it was too dangerous to be joined."

"But it's too dangerous to not be joined," Soli says. "Don't you agree?"

Elsain nods. "But we will have to find a different way. We cannot destroy the necklace."

"How else can we make Andria a faerie?" Soli asks. "That's what it will take."

Elsain says, "I believe there is a way to rejoin the kingdoms in peace."

"What is it?" I ask, impatient. "And can we do it without using Soli's blood?"

Elsain sighs. "Georg has to die."

Chapter 6

Soli

Of course Elsain is right.

Of course we have to kill Georg.

Then Caro will become queen, and she will agree to reunite the kingdoms, and we'll all live happily ever after in a beautiful, peaceful faerieground.

We all look at each other in the throne room.

"I can't kill my father," Caro says finally. "I hate him, he's terrible, but I can't kill him."

Across the table, tears fall down Lucy's face.

"I don't want to be there when it happens,"
Caro says.

"You don't have to be," Kheelan says.

Elsain turns to go. "Wait," I say. "Do you know
what will happen? Don't all Ladybirds know
the future?"

She smiles. "I do," she says. "I cannot tell you
what will happen, but I can tell you that you
will be brave." She looks at my friends. "You all
will be brave." Then she leaves.

We sit in silence in the throne room for a while longer. Then Caro stands. "I can't be here while you make the plan," she says. "And you need to start to make the plan now. We're running out of time."

She leaves, and Kheelan and Lucy and I stare at each other across the table. "I don't want to kill anyone," Lucy says.

Kheelan nods. "That's why I'm the one who has to do it," he says. He gazes into my eyes. "I'm the only one who can, Soli."

Maybe he's right. Maybe he was born to kill the Crow king. But I don't know if I can love a murderer.

"It's the right thing to do," he whispers. "You have to let me do this for Roseland."

"We could just wait until Georg dies of old age," I say. "We can protect Roseland until then, can't we?"

Lucy snorts. "Against those people? No way," she says. "They're vicious."

"Georg might not die for hundreds of years," Kheelan says. "It isn't like your—" He stops. Takes a breath. "It isn't like the human world," he finishes. "We can't wait for him to die."

"Elsain told us what we have to do," I say.

Kheelan nods. "Just leave it to me," he says. "There will be no blood on either of your hands." I look at his strong, gentle hands. How could I love a killer?

He stands. "I'll leave now. Tell Caro to be ready. She'll know when the king is gone."

Chapter 7

Lucy

Kheelan leaves at nightfall, and Soli and Caro and I wait in the queen's quarters.

We don't talk. Soli reads from a book. Caro

sharpens a knife against a long stone. I wait.

I glance at Caro. I know how it feels to lose a

father, but I don't know how it feels to lose a

father like hers. I always knew my dad loved

me. Caro has been fighting for her father's

love for her whole life. That's why she is the

way she is. That's why she's Caro, the Betrayer.

Sitting here now, I guess, while someone goes

to kill her father, is the ultimate betrayal.

Maybe she's tricking us. Maybe she's going to

warn King Georg. Maybe she already has.

Chapter 8

Soli

Hours after Kheelan rode toward the Crows, I look up from Andria's journal.

"Caro," I say. "You never read this?"

She shakes her head.

"Where did you find it?" I ask.

"In the greenhouse room," she tells me.

"Why?"

I look down at Andria's handwriting again, swimming on the page in front of me. "I think we were wrong," I say. "About Andria. But not about Georg."

I read out loud:

Calandra came to me in the night. She told me what she found.

A key to a secret passage, and a room full of evil. Descriptions of my every move. Dark spells. War plans. I didn't believe her, so she showed me.

Georg wants to take over the faerieground. He's a murderer. He and his Crows have killed thousands already. They stop at nothing.

He wasn't lying about turning me into a faerie. There's a spell. It's all written in the books.

Calandra came to me in the night. She told me what she found.

A Key to a secret ~~spy~~ passage, and a room full of evil.

Descriptions of my every move. __Dark__ spells. WAR PLANS.

I didn't believe her, so she showed me.

Georg wants to take over the faerieground. He's a murderer.

He and his Crows have killed thousands already.

__They stop at nothing__

He wasn't lying about ~~her~~ turning me into a faerie.

There's a __spell__. It's all written in the books. To make me full fae he needs the blood of a halfling. The only halfling here is Caro.

__My Daughter.__

will leave tonight. I can't take Caro with me. I don't know the spells to protect a faire in the human world.

Calandria will need to stay behind, so that he doesn't come after me. but she will come home soon.

don't think he'll care that I'm gone. He'll just care that the beloved Crow Queen is gone.

He'll be embarrassed. He wont miss me.

I feel like a fool for not knowing he never loved me.

To make me full faerie, he needs the blood of a halfling. The only halfling here is Caro. My daughter.

I will leave tonight. I can't take Caro with me. I don't know the spells to protect a faerie in the human world.

Calandra will need to stay behind, so that he doesn't come after me, but she will come home soon.

I don't think he'll care that I'm gone. He'll just care that the beloved Crow Queen is gone. He'll be embarrassed. He won't miss me.

I feel like a fool for not knowing he never loved me.

That's the last page in the book.

Lucy and Caro stare at me. "So she's not back to help take over the faerieground?" Caro says finally.

"I think she came back for you," I admit. "And Lucy, of course."

"At least this means we know Kheelan is doing the right thing," Lucy says. "Georg needs to be stopped."

Caro shivers. Then she looks at me. "I think he's gone," she says.

"Did you feel it?" I ask. "Can you tell?"

She nods, and one tear slips from her eye.

We are quiet for a while. After an hour or two, Jonn comes into my rooms, a solemn look on his face.

"We have just received a message from the Crows," he says.

"We know," I say. "Georg is gone."

Jonn nods.

"Is Kheelan okay?" I ask.

He looks confused. "Why do you ask that?" he
says. "Why wouldn't he be?"

Caro and Lucy and I look at each other.
"Because he went to kill Georg," I say slowly.

Jonn shakes his head. "He didn't kill Georg," he
says. "Andria did."

Chapter 9

Soli

She came back to stop Georg and save
her daughters.

And to save me.

Even the Ladybirds were wrong about Andria.

When we find her, hours later, traveling toward Roseland in the forest outside the Crow palace, she is crying and exhausted. She hugs Lucy first, and then stares at Caro.

"Is it you?" Andria whispers. "Caro?"

Caro smiles. "Hello again," she says. "I've missed you." They hug, and Andria steps back to look at both of her daughters.

"We thought you were here to destroy the faerieground," I say. "I'm so sorry."

Andria smiles. "How could you have known?" she asks. "The only person who knew was Calandra. I promised her." Then she turns to Caro. "You're the queen now," she says. "Do what you know is right."

Caro nods, and Lucy smiles. "I forgot!" Lucy says. "Here's your necklace." She takes the blue pendant and slips it over Caro's head. And I can see the queen inside Caro, who no longer is a betrayer.

Chapter 10

Soli

It is over.

After we walk back to Roseland, after the

other kings and queens are gathered, after

the kingdoms have been restored to one

glorious faerieground, after Andria goes home

with Lucy, and after some years have passed,

Kheelan and I will marry. We will have a

daughter, and I will name her Lucy.

I will tell her stories about my childhood,

but we will not cross back over to the human

world. We will seal the borders, so that the

worlds are separate, so that no magic can slip

through the walls.

But even when I'm a thousand years old, I will never forget the first Lucy, my almost-sister, my best friend.

The sun to my shadow.

The girl who believed in me.

Chapter 11

Andria

When I left the faerieground
the first time, I hoped I'd never
have to return.

But when Lucy was taken—when Lucy came home with the Equinox pendant—I knew I'd have to. Georg was still out there and I was the only one who could stop him.

He had a plan to take over the faerieground. When I came back, we were to destroy the necklace and murder the halfling. With the necklace destroyed, the kingdoms couldn't be united. But they could be won.

He's the one who stole the Roseland necklace for me. He's the one who, later, tricked the Ladybirds into giving me Soli.

When I came back to the faerieground I had to pretend as if everything is normal, as if the plan was in effect. I had to screw up my courage and kiss that monster. We had to laugh together and talk about how finally, finally, our time had come. And then, when the sun had set over the Equinox kingdom, and the children had been given time to get away, I had to kill him. I had to slit his throat with his own sword. It was the only way.

I am not a murderer, but I could not let him live in this world. Even if this world is not my own, I have always loved it.

Chapter 12

Lucy

At bedtime, Lina asks for faerie stories.

I tell her tales about Queen Soledad and her husband, King Kheelan. I tell her about Queen Carolin. And I tell her how if she makes a wish in the woods near our house, the faeries might let her slip over to their side. How they used to be cruel, some of them, but now they're kind.

And every night, she asks if I believe in faeries. She asks if the stories are true.

"I don't know," I tell her.

For all I know, they could be.

Beth & Kay

Kay Fraser and *Beth Bracken* are a designer-editor team in Minnesota.

Kay is from Buenos Aires. She left home at eighteen and moved to North Dakota—basically the exact opposite of Argentina. These days, she designs books, writes, makes tea for her husband, and drives their daughters to their dance lessons.

Beth and her husband live in a light-filled house with their son, Sam, and their daughter, Etta. Beth spends her time editing, reading, daydreaming, and rearranging her furniture.

Kay and Beth both love dark chocolate, Buffy, and tea.

Odessa

Odessa Sawyer is an illustrator from Santa Fe, New Mexico. She works mainly in digital mixed media, utilizing digital painting, photography, and traditional pen and ink.

Odessa's work has graced the book covers of many top publishing houses, and she has also done work for various film and television projects, posters, and album covers.

Highly influenced by fantasy, fairy tales, fashion, and classic horror, Odessa's work celebrates a whimsical, dreamy, and vibrant quality.